CW00848382

Race

Val Biro

Published by the Penguin Group
Penguin Books Ltd, 27 Wrights Lane, London
W8 5TZ, England
Penguin Books Australia Ltd, Ringwood,
Victoria, Australia
Penguin Books Canada Ltd, 10 Alcorn Avenue,
Toronto, Ontario, Canada M4V 3B2
Penguin Books (NZ) Ltd, 182-190 Wairau Road,
Auckland 10, New Zealand

Penguin Books Ltd, Registered Offices:
Harmondsworth, Middlesex, England

This edition first published in Great Britain in 1982
by Hodder and Stoughton

This edition published by Claremont Books,
an imprint of Godfrey Cave Associates Limited,
42 Bloomsbury Street, London, WC1B 3QJ,
under licence from Val Biro, 1996

Copyright © 1982 Val Biro

ISBN 1 854 71787 1

Gumdrop, as all the world knows, is a beautiful old car. But one of his best friends is even older. Her name is Swanscombe, and people call her Swanny for short. She is a green steam-engine. Old or not, she is just as lively on the railway-line as Gumdrop is on the road.

One day Mr Oldcastle spoke to Swanny's driver.

'I say, Bill, how about having a race between your Swanny and my Gumdrop? The road and the line run side by side to Quainton Station. Let's see which of us gets there first!'

'That's fine by me,' said Bill, 'as long as we don't exceed 40 miles per hour.' So they agreed, and the race was on.

On the following Sunday they lined up side by side. There were three passengers in Gumdrop (not forgetting Horace, the dog), and three in Swanny's tender. When Mr Oldcastle gave the signal: HONK, HONK, Swanny replied TOOT, TOOT, the passengers raised a cheer and the great race began.

Gumdrop was the first to get going, because it takes longer for a steam-engine to start. Soon he was well ahead, but not for long: a lumbering slow car held him up. But Swanny had got up speed by then and she steamed busily past with a loud TOOT!

It took some time for Gumdrop to overtake the lumbering car, and Swanny was well ahead by then. But not for long: the signal was against her! So she had to stop, and Gumdrop came merrily past with a loud HONK!

Swanny had to wait, chuffing and puffing, until the signal changed, and Gumdrop was so far ahead that he had disappeared round a corner. But there the road crossed the line and the gate was closed! So Gumdrop had to stop and watch as Swanny chugged cheerfully past! TOOTLE-TOOT!

By the time the gate opened, Swanny was so far ahead that she disappeared round another corner. But there the road crossed the line again and the gate was closed against her! So this time Swanny had to stop and watch helplessly as Gumdrop crossed in front of her, with a HONKETY-HONK!

When the gate opened at last, Swanny got up speed and clattered quickly after Gumdrop. Soon she caught up with him, too, and there were no more signals or gates. The line and the road ran side by side, and they were racing neck and neck. And there was Quainton Station ahead! Who will get there first?

Just then Swanny made a funny noise. HUFF-HUFF, CHUFF-CHUFF, PUFFFFF. What was worse, she began to slow down! Bill turned the handles, pulled the knobs and shifted the levers. But it was no good. Swanny had run out of steam!

At the same time Gumdrop made some funny noises too. BRRRM-BRRRM, GURGLE-GURGLE, GLUGGGGG. What was worse, he began to slow down as well! Mr Oldcastle pressed the accelerator, retarded the magneto and pulled out the choke. But it was no good. Gumdrop had run out of petrol!

Swanny and Gumdrop were both slowing down, rolling along side by side. And there was the station straight in front of them! The passengers jumped up and down to make their machines roll a little faster, but it was no good: Swanny and Gumdrop came to a stop at exactly the same moment. And they were still side by side as they reached the station at last.

Everybody cheered the two winners.
Gumdrop and Swanny were each as
good as the other!